To Eliot and Manon

First published 2009 by Walker Books Ltd
87 Vauxhall Walk, London SE11 5HJ

10 9 8 7 6 5 4 3 2 1

This book has been typeset in Futura

Printed in China

British Library Cataloguing in Publication Data:
a catalogue record for this book is available from the British Library

ISBN 978-1-4063-2065-7

www.walker.co.uk

Suzy Goose
and the
Christmas
Star

Petr Horáček

WALKER BOOKS
AND SUBSIDIARIES
LONDON · BOSTON · SYDNEY · AUCKLAND

It was Christmas Eve.
Suzy Goose and her friends
were gathered around the tree.

It was beautiful.
But it was missing one thing.

"It needs a star on top," honked Suzy. "Just like the one in the sky. I'll get it."

And before anybody
could stop her,
Suzy dived off the
top of the hill.

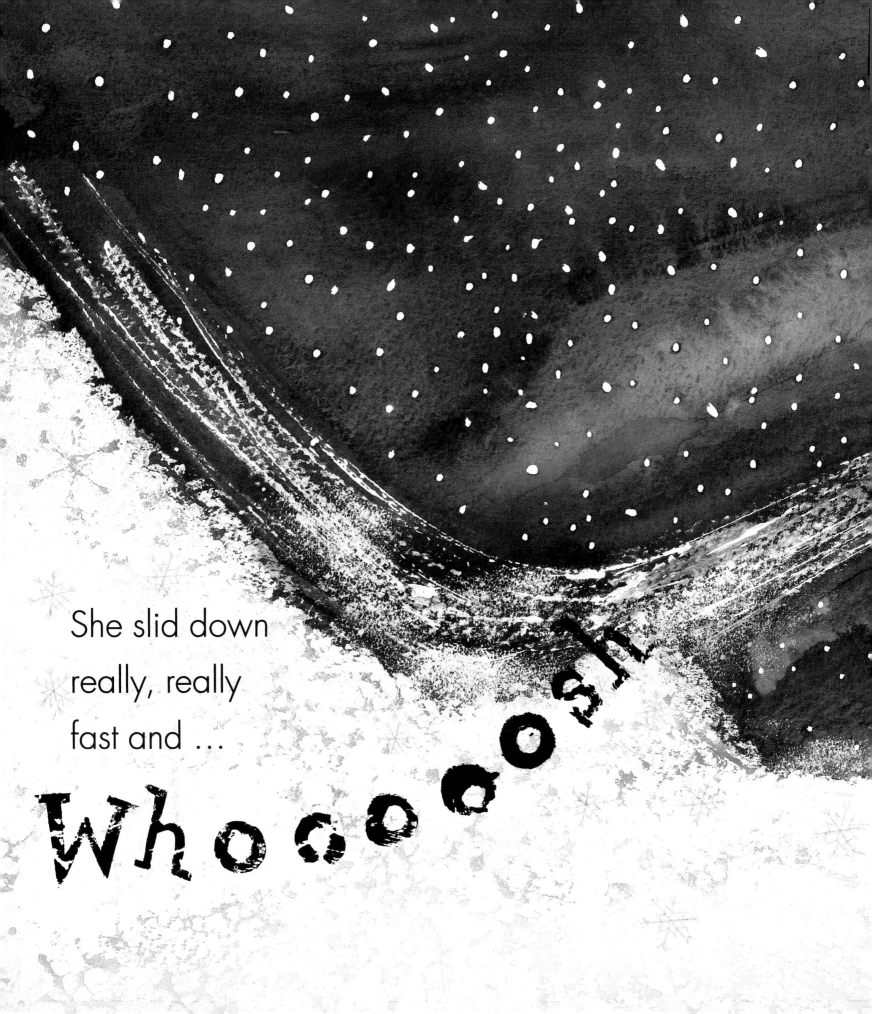

She slid down
really, really
fast and ...

Whoooooosh

flew high up in the sky.

But not quite
high enough.

Splat!

"Never mind," honked Suzy.

"I have another plan."

She saw
a fence,

climbed
on top,

stretched up
very, very high
and ...
jumped.

But not quite
high enough.

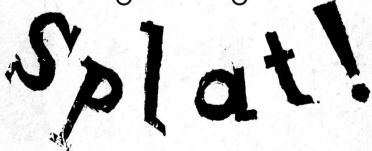

"Never mind,"
thought Suzy.
"I'll try again."
She saw a pile of logs,

climbed
on top,

stretched up
very, very high
and ...
jumped.

But not quite
high enough.
Splat!

"Never mind," thought Suzy.
She decided to walk towards the star.

The wind was blowing.
The snow was falling.
It was getting late.

Suzy walked and walked and walked.
She was tired.
"It's Christmas Eve, I can't reach the star
and I'm very far from my friends,"
she thought.

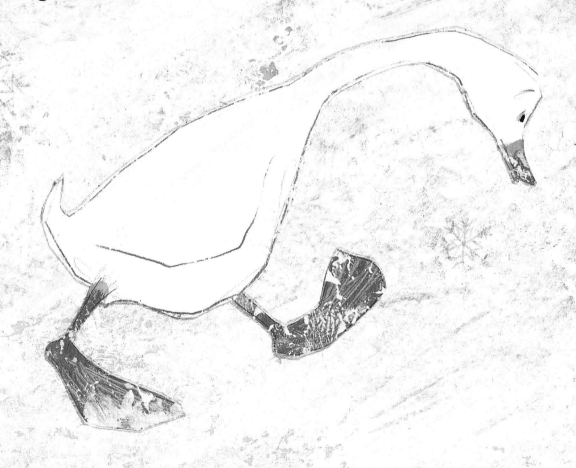

Suzy Goose was alone.
She was lost.

Then she heard a familiar sound
in the distance.

Ding

Honk Ding

Honk

"I know that sound!" honked Suzy happily.

"The sound is coming from my friends.

Ding

Honk

They are
calling me!"

Ding

Honk

and
she ran
towards it.

Moo
Moo

Oink
Oink

Suzy's friends were so
glad to see her.
How nice it was to be back!
Everybody made happy noises.

Then she noticed that some of the geese were staring up at the sky.

And when Suzy turned around,
she saw the beautiful star
shining right above the tree
after all.

It looked magical!

"Happy Christmas," honked Suzy Goose
with all her friends.